AMERICAN INDIANS

in America

AMERICAN INDIANS

Volume 2: The Late 18th Century to the Present

Jayne Clark Jones

 Lerner Publications Company • Minneapolis

Front cover: The Littlesun family of the Northern Cheyenne gather to take part in a Pow-wow on the Northern Cheyenne Reservation near Lame Deer, Montana.

Page 2: Three women and one man of the Ute tribe were photographed in the late 19th century as they rode through a birch forest in Utah.

LIBRARY OF CONGRESS CATALOGING-IN-PUBLICATION DATA

Jones, Jayne Clark.
  American Indians in America.
  (The In America series)
  Rev. ed. of: The American Indian in America. 1973.
  Includes index.
  Volume titles on cover.
  Contents: v. 1. Prehistory to the late 18th century —
v. 2. The late 18th century to the present.
  1. Indians of North America—Juvenile literature. [1. Indians of North America.] I. Jones, Jayne Clark. American Indian in America. II. Title. III. Series.
  ISBN 0-8225-1951-8 (lib. bdg. : v. 1) — ISBN 0-8225-1047-2 (pbk. : v. 1) — ISBN 0-8225-0240-2 (lib. bdg. : v. 2) — ISBN 0-8225-1037-5 (pbk. : v. 2)
E77.4.J66 1991   90-13419
973'.0497—dc20   CIP
                                                            AC

Manufactured in the United States of America

2 3 4 5 6 7 8 9 10 00 99 98 97 96 95 94 93 92

CONTENTS

1
FROM SEA TO SHINING SEA

Totem poles carved from huge ever-green trees were important in most of the Indian cultures of the Pacific Northwest. These Indians near Sitka, Alaska, carry on the tradition of carving totem poles by hand.

A Group of Many Peoples

In 1783, when the Treaty of Paris ended the American Revolutionary War, the newly formed United States took official possession of a huge chunk of North America. At least it was official according to European rules. But other people who played by different rules actually lived on the land—people who had not been invited to the peace conference. These were the American Indians.

Recent genetic research has suggested that most of America's modern Indians are descended from only a few original immigrants from Asia to North America. By the 16th century, however, the original peoples of North America had diversified greatly and had formed hundreds of identifiable tribes. Some of these tribes had closely related languages and cultures. Others were more culturally different from one another than Arabs were from Swedes. If Europeans had never arrived in North America, there might never have been any need to bunch together such diverse peoples as the Tlingits of the Pacific Northwest and the Havasupais of Arizona.

But the Europeans did arrive. Circumstances forged a group out of vastly different tribes, a group that needed a name. The term *Indians* survives from Christopher Columbus's mistaken belief that his ships had reached the East Indies. As illogical as the term is, it remains the most common group name for the people whose ancestors populated the Americas before the Europeans arrived. Most American Indians, while they may like to point out exactly which tribe they belong to, do not mind being called Indians. Another term, *Native Americans*, is also widely used and is generally acceptable as another name for American Indians.

About 7 million Americans have reported having at least one American Indian ancestor. This makes the category of American Indians one of the largest of all reported ancestral groups in this country. Far fewer persons (not quite 2 million) listed American Indian ancestry without mentioning some other ethnic background mixed in as well. The states that have the greatest numbers of residents of pure American Indian descent are Oklahoma and Texas.

In Alaska, a special distinction is made between American Indians and two other peoples, the Inuit (often called Eskimos) and the Aleuts. The Inuit and the Aleuts inhabited Alaska long before Europeans arrived, but these two peoples did not settle in North America until about 10,000 years ago. The ancestors of the American Indians had arrived long before that, probably between 30,000 and 40,000 years ago.

The American Indians have not had an easy life in the United States. Individual Americans have robbed them, cheated them, murdered them, and shut them out of many mainstream activities. The United States government has been insensitive, inconsistent, warlike, paternalistic, and dishonest—often all at the same time—to them. Even late in the 20th century, with somewhat lower barriers to their success, American Indians have had to struggle mightily to claim their rights as U.S. citizens.

Despite these obstacles, American Indians are not permanently downtrodden and helpless. Through hard work and careful planning, they have been improving their conditions. Some have won greater power to govern themselves. Others have gone to court to win back some of their stolen land. Some have succeeded—as outstanding politicians, writers, athletes, or artists—in terms recognizable to European-descended Americans. Others enjoy a lower-profile success defined by more traditional tribal values. Each of these success stories illustrates the exceptional strength and resilience of the American Indians.

Manifest Destiny

To many 18th-century thinkers, Britain's American colonies offered a unique chance to create a truly democratic nation. Such leaders as Benjamin Franklin, Thomas Jefferson, and John Adams shared this belief. After independence had been declared, these leaders were determined not to transplant Europe's old, aristocratic political systems to the new country. The laws of the United States would protect the common good and human rights. No one would be deprived of life, liberty, or property without due process of law.

Still, despite their support for these ideals, Americans discovered that democratic principles often conflicted with national and personal ambitions. The American Indians presented an especially difficult problem. Did they have the same rights as European Americans? If Indians were given guarantees of life, liberty, and (especially) property, how could the United States expand?

Not all European Americans were insensitive to Indian rights. Some non-Indian Americans thought that the United States could live up to its ideals only by respecting the Indians as equals with the whites and all other human beings. Others were unwilling to stretch democracy that far.

European Americans devised many excuses for mistreating the Indians and allowing the government to mistreat them. Indians are not human at

Sacajawea, a Shoshone woman, guided the Lewis and Clark Expedition across much of the western territory acquired by the United States in the Louisiana Purchase.

all, some claimed, so Indians are not entitled to human rights. Indians are not citizens, others said, so Indians are not entitled to the rights of citizens. Many Americans over the generations took refuge in the idea that God had a special plan for white people to rule North America. According to this racist belief, if Indians lost their land and their lives at the hands of whites, it was only because God wanted it that way.

Almost as soon as there was a United States of America, Americans began to envision the new nation spanning the continent, from the Atlantic to the Pacific. Many Americans even believed in an idea called *manifest destiny*—that the United States was predestined to expand westward to the Pacific. By encompassing all the land between the oceans, the United States would only be fulfilling God's plan. A lot of Indians, however, lived between the Atlantic and the Pacific.

A British proclamation in 1763, before the Revolutionary War, had prohibited white settlement west of the Appalachians. The country to the west was to be preserved as a hunting ground for the Indians. But settlers were never bothered by this restriction. European Americans were moving into Kentucky and the Ohio Valley even before the Revolution. More territory was opened up for white expansion in 1784 and 1785, when various tribes ceded large parcels of land in the Northwest Territory to the newly formed United States. In 1785, Thomas Jefferson devised a plan for surveying and selling the new territory for the profit of his government, which was in bad financial shape. This plan was adopted as the Ordinance of 1785. In the section of the ordinance that set up rules for the admission of states, new state governments were advised to observe "good faith" toward the Indians.

The federal government's own commitment to "good faith," however, seemed weak. By 1802, all the states had ceded their western lands to the federal government. When North Carolina gave up its claim to certain territory west of the Appalachian Mountains, the state stopped making payments that had earlier been guaranteed to the Indians of that region. The United States was supposed to pay the debt but never did.

The United States expanded at an almost incredible pace. In 1803, the United States bought the immense Louisiana territory from France, a purchase that extended the nation's western border to the Rocky Mountains.

In 1819, Florida was purchased by the United States from Spain. Texas, which had been settled by slave-owning American cotton growers, won its independence from Mexico in 1836 and was annexed as an American state in 1845. After U.S. troops won the Mexican War in 1848, the area from California to the boundaries of Texas became U.S. territory. The U.S. and Great Britain agreed upon the northern boundary of Maine in 1842 and the northern border of the Oregon Territory in 1846. By 1854 – only 78 years after the colonies had declared their independence from Great Britain – U.S. territory extended across the continent. Manifest destiny, it seemed, had been fulfilled.

The Removal of the Eastern Tribes

Settlers rushed into the newly acquired territories, but the Indians did, indeed, get in the way. Americans eager to claim new land and new resources expected the government to do something about the "Indian problem." Genocide (the elimination of an entire ethnic group) is a grisly concept. Many Americans in the 19th century, however, said publicly and in print that the best solution to the "Indian problem" was extermination. This was not official government policy; the government never admitted anything but good intentions towards the Indians. Still, the relationship between the government and the Indians was characterized more by conflict and war than by peace and cooperation.

The War of 1812

Even though the British had agreed to leave the Northwest Territory after the Revolution, they continued to

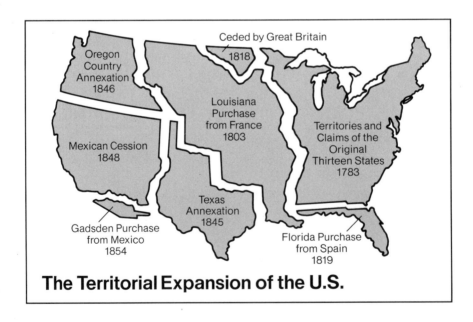

The Territorial Expansion of the U.S.

Ceded by Great Britain 1818

Oregon Country Annexation 1846

Louisiana Purchase from France 1803

Territories and Claims of the Original Thirteen States 1783

Mexican Cession 1848

Gadsden Purchase from Mexico 1854

Texas Annexation 1845

Florida Purchase from Spain 1819

maintain several fur-trading posts (which also served as military establishments) in the area. Since a settled country would mean the end of the fur trade, which both the British and the Indians wanted to preserve, the British did nothing to stop Indian attacks on American settlers coming into the territory. Americans were convinced that the British were actually directing the activities of the Indians.

As this conflict worsened, the brilliant and charismatic Tecumseh rose to leadership in the Shawnee tribe. The Shawnees are an Algonquian people, but they lived mostly near the southwestern reaches of the Ohio River, southwest of usual Algonquian territory. Tecumseh was able to express the frustration and outrage felt by the tribes living east of the Mississippi.

Tecumseh planned to unite all Indians in an alliance that could put a stop to the white invasion. He also dreamed of an independent Indian nation north of the Ohio River. He asked two things of his allies: that they refuse to sell any more land and that they delay all military action against whites until the Indian alliance was strong enough to be effective. Tecumseh's emissaries carried his proposal as far away as the Missouri River, and he himself made several long trips to try to enlist tribes of the East and Southeast.

Attempts to form confederations of tribes had been unsuccessful in the

Tecumseh

past, but Tecumseh was an altogether unusual person. He was a steadfast fighter, but he was also compassionate and humane. If he discovered that any of his followers had tortured a prisoner, he would fly into a rage and banish anyone responsible for such cruelty.

Besides being a skilled speaker, Tecumseh had another advantage: his younger brother Tenskwatawa, known as the Shawnee Prophet, was a religious leader who had made several accurate prophecies. Tenskwatawa's presence gave Tecumseh's whole movement a religious aspect that most Indians took very seriously.

Tecumseh had a practical plan of resistance and was able to convince many tribes to join him. The fatal flaw in his scheme, however, was that it depended too greatly on Tecumseh's own personal leadership. In order to ensure its success, Tecumseh had to go from tribe to tribe explaining and selling his plan. In many cases, he had to convince traditional enemies to be allies. Tecumseh had no time to train other reliable leaders who could help him hold the alliance together, and the job was physically impossible for one person.

Even before the War of 1812 broke out, American, British, and Indian forces skirmished occasionally. One of these battles, a brief raid in 1811

known as the Battle of Tippecanoe, dealt a severe blow to Tecumseh's plan. William Henry Harrison led his U.S. forces against Tenskwatawa's village beside the Tippecanoe River in Indiana and scattered the Indians. Not many people were killed, but the Indian defeat demolished the myth of the Shawnee Prophet's magic.

The Indians' alliance with the British in the Northwest Territory also proved to be a mixed blessing. It drew Tecumseh and his Indian followers into military action before they were ready. By 1813, the British were retreating from American territory toward Canada. Tenskwatawa's old foe, William Henry Harrison, overtook and defeated the British and their Indian allies near the

Seminoles usually built their houses on stilts to keep them dry.

Thames River in Canada. Tecumseh was killed in the battle, and the Indian confederacy died with him.

The War of 1812 also created problems for the Indians of the southeastern United States. During colonial times, the so-called "civilized" tribes of the Southeast—the Choctaws, Cherokees, Creeks, and Chickasaws (and, later, the Seminoles)—had managed to prosper. The Creeks, a group of related tribes living in Georgia, Alabama, and northern Florida, had been especially successful in their alliance with the British. Trade had been profitable, and many Creeks became wealthy. Creek villages were strongly agricultural, and many Creeks came to own large herds of cattle; as time passed, the Creeks' way of life grew more and more like that of their white neighbors.

Before the Revolution, the Creeks were valuable to the British as a buffer that separated the British colony at Charleston from the French in New Orleans and the Spanish in Florida. When the British left after the Revolution, the Creeks were under constant pressure from American settlers. Raiding between Indian and white settlements was frequent.

Many Creeks and other Indians who were accused of crimes or who were refugees of raids escaped to Spanish Florida, where Americans could not follow. They took refuge among other fugitives in the swamps. These inhabitants of the swamps became known as the Seminoles—one of the "civilized"

tribes of the Southeast. Americans, particularly those on the frontier, were immensely annoyed that they were not allowed to pursue their Indian enemies into Spanish Florida. The threat of an Indian alliance with either the Spanish or the British was feared by many Americans, and with good cause.

Although some Creeks did not want war, a much larger group was hostile to the United States and was won over to Tecumseh's plan. These Indians agreed to postpone raiding and other hostilities against Americans until the signal should come for a united Indian attack. But when they learned that America was again preparing for war with the British, they began to hope that they might help defeat the Americans and thus restore the colonial balance of power. It was at this time that a prowar party of Creeks made an official visit to the Spanish governor in Pensacola, presumably to discuss an alliance with the Spanish. On their way home, the Creeks were attacked by a group of whites. In August 1813, the Indians retaliated by attacking Fort Mims in the Mississippi Territory, where white settlers, expecting a British assault, had gathered for protection. The Indians easily overran the stockade and massacred all but a few of those inside.

When the Fort Mims massacre took place, General Andrew Jackson and his troops—one of the many American militias organized in expectation of war with the British—were still in Tennessee, waiting for a military assignment. Now they had an objective. Jackson was an experienced, shrewd, tough, and ruthless fighter. He marched his troops into Creek territory and fought several battles against the Creeks in late 1813 and early 1814. In March 1814, he attacked a large force of Creeks at Horseshoe Bend on the Tallapoosa River in Georgia. Jackson defeated the Creeks, killing 550 of them. Creek power was broken, and most of the Creek warriors and their families fled to Florida. The pro-American Indians who stayed behind were starving as a result of the war. Jackson took advantage of their weakness and demanded the cession of a tract of land that included one-fifth of Georgia and three-fifths of what came to be Alabama.

Jackson's defeat of the Creeks won him the command of all American military action in the South—a command he held when he defeated the British in the famous Battle of New Orleans. By advertising his military successes, Jackson embarked on a political career. The death of Tecumseh and the rise of Andrew Jackson as a national figure meant hard times ahead for the American Indians living east of the Mississippi.

Andrew Jackson, who became the seventh president of the United States, pursued harsh policies against American Indians.

The Trail of Tears

Andrew Jackson, the new American hero, became president of the United States in 1828. Americans on the frontier admired Jackson and expected great things of him. One thing they expected and got was a harsh, unyielding policy towards Indians.

The Cherokees, neighbors of the Creeks in the Southeast, were among the first victims of Jackson's Indian policy. The Cherokees had been friendly to the first white colonists in Georgia. During the colonial period, they allied

In this painting by Robert Lindneux, Cherokees march westward along the Trail of Tears. Even though the U.S. Supreme Court ruled that the Cherokees should not be removed from their homes, President Jackson sent U.S. troops to force them out.

themselves with whichever nation offered them the best deal, but, like the Creeks, they most often sided with the British. Throughout the colonial period, the Cherokee lands were settled by whites. From time to time, the Indians gave up some of their land in treaties with the British crown or with the colonies.

The Cherokees supported the British during the Revolutionary War. After the Revolution, the American government told the Cherokees that it expected nothing from them but their loyalty. The people of Georgia, however, did want something else—the Cherokees' land—and they proceeded to take it. The Cherokees were persuaded several times to give up title to various tracts of land.

In spite of their continuing troubles with white settlers, the Cherokees managed to thrive on the lands that remained to them. An independent Cherokee Nation was established in 1827—a thoroughly credible state with a constitution and a representative form of government. They had productive fields, large herds, thriving trade with New Orleans, schools, and a newspaper. This newspaper (the *Cherokee Phoenix*) and the Cherokee constitution could be written in the Cherokee language because a Cherokee genius, Sequoyah, had finished devising a Cherokee writing system in 1821. This remarkable system—the first to represent an Indian language without simply forcing a European alphabet around it—made literacy common among the Cherokees.

But the state of Georgia claimed jurisdiction over all its residents and denied the sovereignty of the Cherokee Nation. White raids against the Indians went unchecked. Indians were tried and punished for crimes against whites, but Indian testimony was not even allowed in Georgia courts. Time after time, the Cherokees appealed to the federal government to keep its treaty obligations and protect them and their lands. But the War Department, which was responsible for protecting the Indians, said that the white squatters (people who had simply grabbed Cherokee land without any legal right to it) were too numerous to be moved. Instead, the department pressured the Indians to cede land again and again. Finally, the Cherokees went to the Supreme Court of the United States seeking justice.

The Court upheld the Cherokee position. Numerous illustrious American leaders, such as Daniel Webster and Henry Clay, also supported the Cherokees. President Jackson, however, made no more effort to enforce the decision of the Court than he had made to enforce earlier treaties. Instead,

Jackson and the Congress decided to solve the problem by "removing" the Indians from the area and sending them to the West.

This was colossal ignorance and insensitivity. Cultures based upon the crops and animals of the eastern woodlands could not be kept intact on the prairie. People forced to move to entirely new climates found themselves without even such simple survival skills as the ability to make appropriate clothing. Such transported tribes suffered greatly because they lacked immunity to the diseases prevalent in the new areas to which they had been moved.

Nonetheless, as early as 1825, Vice President John C. Calhoun suggested that the government pursue a policy of removal. In 1830, when the U.S. Congress passed the Indian Removal Act, this infamous policy became law. In preparation for removal, an Indian Territory was laid out in what is now Oklahoma. Indians were ordered to leave their ancestral homes in the East and move westward along what became known as the Trail of Tears.

The Choctaws left first, in 1831. The Creeks managed to delay for four years and were finally moved by force; those who resisted made the journey in chains. The Chickasaws left in 1837. The Cherokees, who had already spent many bitter years fighting for their homeland, continued to resist. Once more they appealed to the Supreme Court, and once more the Court ruled in favor of the Cherokees. The final cession of Cherokee lands had been obtained by fraud, the Court ruled, and the Cherokee Nation was justified in refusing to leave. But President Jackson, ignoring the Court's ruling, sent troops to force the Cherokees to leave their homes. In the end, although some Cherokees managed to hide away in the mountains of North Carolina, the Cherokee Nation agreed to go.

The government had financed the removal of other tribes, but the Cherokees were forced to pay for being evicted from their own land. On foot, by wagon and boat, prodded by the military, without sufficient supplies or funds, the Cherokees moved west. They were harassed along the way by whites who stole their goods and animals and who continually threatened violence. They suffered from cholera when their route took them through country where an epidemic raged. Still, U.S. troops drove them on regardless of disease, weather, or the suffering of the people from hunger and exposure. Nearly one-fourth of the Cherokees died on the way. In all, about 100,000 Cherokees, Choctaws, Creeks, and Chickasaws were removed to the Indian Territory along the Trail of Tears.

The Seminoles in Florida were to be next. They fought fiercely, however, and managed to keep the army in a costly and embarrassing war until 1842. Finally some Seminoles surrendered and were moved west to the Indian Territory, but a few hung on in the swamps until the troops gave up and left them in peace.

Black Hawk's Resistance

So it went everywhere east of the Mississippi. In 1804, the Sauks and Foxes had been swindled out of their land in Illinois by William Henry Harrison, the governor of the Indiana Territory. Americans were eager to have the support of the Sauks and Foxes and other midwestern tribes during the War of 1812. But, once the British threat had been removed, the Indians were pressed to abandon their lands on the east side of the river. One group of Sauks, led by a chief named Keokuk, agreed to move west of the Mississippi and received a parcel of land in Iowa. Other Sauks, led by Chief Black Hawk, were determined to stay. In spite of white attacks, they returned each year to their village at Rock Island, Illinois, to plant their crops. Then, in July of 1832, U.S. troops chased them across the river, killing 200 or more men, women, and children.

The Winning of the West

The early belief that whites would not be interested in settling the grasslands of the Great Plains soon changed. Americans began to travel west, seeking trade with the Mexicans in the

American Indians found their way of life disrupted by the coming of the railroads to the West. Even on semi-arid land such as this, the railroads disturbed pastures.

Southwest and with the Indians in the Oregon Territory. Once the Santa Fe Trail and the Oregon Trail—two major westward routes—had been established, American settlers moved through the difficult terrain to settle in California and Oregon. Soon people realized that the land between the Mississippi and the Rockies was not worthless. When gold was discovered in California in 1849, the trickle of travelers became a flood, and many new trails were opened.

During the 1840s, the American government changed its policy regarding the sale of public lands. Instead of surveying new lands before they were sold, the government opened new territory to anyone who agreed to live on and improve a piece of property. These squatters were allowed free use of the land and acquired the right to buy it for the minimum price when it was offered for sale. Naturally, this policy encouraged settlement in the West.

Wherever the travelers and settlers went, the army moved ahead, establishing forts and garrisons for the protection of the invading whites. During the Civil War, few troops were available for western posts; this led to a lull in the westward movement, since whites did not care to push into Indian country without protection. But when the war was over, the army came back, opening new roads in the West and protecting the whites who used them.

Railroad builders were also moving into the West with the aid and encouragement of the government. Between 1850 and 1860, railroads received 20 million acres of public land. With the security of public support, they had pushed beyond the Mississippi by 1855. The army cleared Indians out of the lands set aside for railroads.

An End to Treaties

Even in those expansionist times, the U.S. government wanted to make the taking of Indian land seem controlled and legal. Treaties between the U.S. government and the Indians provided the necessary legal window-dressing. During the 19th century, the American government made separate treaties with each Indian tribe, a practice that had been established by the European powers during colonial times. Between 1778 and 1871, the federal government made 389 treaties with American Indians.

A treaty is an agreement between one nation and another. By making a treaty with an Indian tribe, the U.S. government was acting as if it considered the tribe a separate, self-governing nation. In fact, that was the government's position until 1871—that the Indian tribes were separate nations. The terms of the treaties, however, were not the usual terms of agreements between sovereign nations.

The Indians almost always had to acknowledge the right of the U.S. government to rule over the Indians' territory, even the land that the Indians kept for themselves. These reserved lands—known as reservations—would not be taxed by the government, but they were still considered U.S. territory. The rest of the land, that which was removed from Indian control, was paid for by the United States government with money and supplies provided in yearly installments. Everything the Indians needed to become farmers on the reservations was to be provided by the U.S. government. Usually, the government also promised funds for teachers who would "civilize" the Indians. In all, the Native Americans gave up a total of nearly a billion acres (405 million hectares) of land by treaty—for a price that averaged under 10 cents an acre.

The United States government and U.S. citizens had no more right to break a treaty with, for example, the Cherokees than with the British, but treaties were broken almost as soon as they were made. Wagon trains of white settlers invaded Indian lands. In retaliation, Indian raiding parties harassed and attacked white settlers. Livestock and supplies were stolen and destroyed. The victims of these raids protested their innocence and maintained that, as peaceful American citizens, they ought to be protected in their own country. Most settlers believed that retaliation would teach the Indians not to meddle with whites. Private citizens regularly took revenge against any Indians who were handy, whether or not they were guilty of any crime.

The Indians were enraged by the behavior of white settlers, who continually trespassed on Indian lands that had been reserved by treaty. The whites showed little respect for the land. They burned and destroyed grass and trees; they wastefully slaughtered game or drove it away. Whites killed innocent Indians without provocation and were insulting and disrespectful

The bones of recently slaughtered American bison lay stacked up beside a railroad track on the prairie in 1887.

20

towards Indian burial grounds and other things the Indians considered sacred. The Indians, to protect their land from destructive whites, often attacked innocent parties. The cycle of blood and violence was hard to break.

By 1871, the U.S. government had grown impatient with the constant Indian wars in the West. It was clear that the treaties were not producing the intended results. The Plains tribes were not turning their ponies into plow horses and settling down as farmers. When it became difficult to find game, the Indians went to the reservations for supplies, especially during the winter months. But when the game reappeared, they left again to hunt on the prairies. They were encouraged to desert the reservations by Indians who had never accepted reservation life. The tribes of the Great Plains were generally content to hunt in peace, but clashes with whites became more frequent as the increasingly large white population demanded protection and more land.

In order to meet these demands, the government decided on a new policy. There were to be no more treaties, and the Indian nations were no longer to be regarded as independent powers. Hostile Indians, moreover, were to be captured by the army and confined to reservations. (Eventually, all Indians who refused to be confined were considered hostile.) To make it easier to confine the Indians, the government helped to destroy their livelihood on the prairies. Wholesale slaughter of American bison was encouraged. Whites shot the animals for fun; hide cutters stripped off the hides and wastefully left the carcasses to rot. Between 1872 and 1874, nearly 4 million bison were killed—all but 150,000 of them by white hunters.

Hardships of Reservation Life

It is not surprising that many tribes resisted being moved to reservations. Even some whites were shocked when they saw the places where Indians were expected to live. Most of the reservations were wastelands so undesirable that no whites wanted them. Indians were often expected to farm land that was totally unsuitable for agriculture. In addition, they were often sent to reservations far from home and in strange climates—desert people to Florida, mountain tribes to the desert. Poor living conditions and disease caused thousands of deaths on the reservations. By the 1870s, the reservations had become a national scandal.

Since 1824, the Bureau of Indian Affairs (BIA) had overseen U.S. government dealings with the Indians. (At first the BIA was part of the Department of War, but it was transferred in 1842 to the newly created Department of the Interior.) BIA agents on Indian reservations often earned their jobs simply by being friends with powerful politicians. Dishonest agents often got rich by cheating both the government and the Indians.

They used many tricks to do this. Some agents kept the names of dead or nonexistent Indians on reservation rolls in order to get higher allowances from the government. Other agents could arrange to buy cheap, inferior supplies so that they spent less than the government had given them for these purchases. The agents kept the remainder. Agents could also profit by spending government money on supplies, reselling what they had bought, and allowing the Indians to go without. In the Southwest, it was often said that BIA agents threw supplies at a ladder, and the Indians got everything that stuck to the rungs; the corrupt agents took everything that fell through.

Plains Indians and Wounded Knee

Many Plains Indians tried reservation life, found it intolerable, and left. Some tribes then formed temporary alliances in efforts to save themselves and their lands. Various branches of the Sioux and Cheyenne were often allies, and great military leaders arose among them: Red Cloud, Crow King, Spotted Tail, Crazy Horse, Gall, and Sitting Bull, who were Sioux; Dull Knife, Little Wolf, and Two Moons, who were Cheyenne. These Plains leaders became famous for their war exploits and often defeated large and well-equipped white armies. They became symbols of Indian resistance for white Americans as well as for their own people. But such triumphs as the defeat of General George A. Custer at the Little Bighorn in 1876 only redoubled the efforts of the army against the Indians. Indian leaders were hunted down and destroyed one by one, and their people were starved into submission.

The Indians who remained free found it more and more difficult to elude the army. The army routinely—even in winter—destroyed the tipis (large portable dwellings made of animal skins and long poles) and the food reserves of any Indians whom they defeated in battle. Then the soldiers usually killed or chased away the Indians' ponies. In their eagerness to show that resistance would not be tolerated, the army sometimes killed innocent Indians.

In their despair, the Indians listened to the promises of a visionary prophet named Wovoka, a member of Nevada's Paiute tribe. Wovoka taught that when the Messiah, God's messenger, had come to earth, whites had abused and killed him. But the Messiah had now returned as an Indian, Wovoka himself. He promised his people that the whites would soon disappear, that the prairie grass would grow tall again, that the buffalo would come back, and that the dead relatives of the Indians would return strong and well. Indians would then live together in peace and plenty.

Wovoka (left) was photographed in 1926 in Nevada with a white resident named T. J. McCoy.

In the late 1880s, Wovoka taught the Indians a dance—the Ghost Dance—that would help them get a glimpse of this new world and would speed up the world's rebirth. Eventually, the Indians came to believe that the shirts worn in the Ghost Dance would protect them from the bullets of the whites.

The Ghost Dance spread all over the Great Plains among Indian people who hoped that their time of suffering would soon pass. Whites, however, saw a threat in the Ghost Dance, and it was forbidden in territory supervised by the BIA.

In 1889, a terrible drought hit the Great Plains, ruining crops and killing many cattle. The government cut back on the amount of beef it would give to Indians on the reservations, and the starving Sioux suffered a deadly epidemic of measles. All these miseries

23

came on top of a major loss of land by the Sioux as the U.S. government opened up more than half of their reservation territory in the Dakotas for white settlement.

Wovoka's prophecies offered some hope for the desperate Sioux, but tragedy was in the air. Numerous Sioux leaders, such as Red Cloud and Big Foot, advocated peace with the whites, but one major leader, Sitting Bull, did not. Sitting Bull, whose original name was Tatanka Iyotake, was a Hunkpapa Sioux who had been one of the leaders of the Sioux and Cheyenne forces against Custer at the Little Bighorn in the mid-1870s. In 1890, Sitting Bull was living at the Standing Rock Reservation (which was partly in North Dakota and partly in South Dakota), and hundreds of excitable Ghost Dancers had gathered to be near him. Worried that Sitting Bull might be preparing to leave the reservation and stir up trouble, U.S. marshals went into the reservation in December and arrested him. Sitting Bull's followers resisted, and in the ensuing battle, Sitting Bull and seven other Indians were killed.

Elsewhere in the Dakotas, Big Foot's group of Ghost Dancers was being herded by U.S. troops towards the Pine

A circle of Ghost Dancers was depicted in this painting by Mary Irvin Wright.

Burying the dead after the Battle of Wounded Knee, S.D. -1890.

After the Wounded Knee Massacre, U.S. troops buried many Indian bodies in a mass grave.

Ridge Reservation in South Dakota. Despite the humiliation of being driven like cattle, Big Foot's people were peaceful and were planning to surrender their guns to government agents once they had reached Pine Ridge. This orderly march, however, ended in one of the most shameful massacres in U.S. history.

Sitting Bull had been killed, and the Indians were nervous. On December 29, 1890, as Big Foot's followers camped at Wounded Knee Creek in South Dakota, they saw U.S. troops encircling

their camp and setting up light cannon. The colonel in charge of these troops, George A. Forsyth, went into camp to confiscate the Indians' weapons straight away. A Ghost Dancer started dancing and shouting, and then a gun went off. Some accounts say that this shot struck one of the U.S. government officers. Other accounts say that the shot flew harmlessly into the air. In either case, it touched off a frenzied, confused battle. The Ghost Dancers, believing that magic made their shirts bulletproof, rose to their feet, but most of them had no guns. Government forces overreacted and began mowing down unarmed women and children with a rain of bullets and cannon shells. The warriors tried to fight back with knives, sticks, and any other makeshift weapons they could find, but they were clearly no match for the well-armed troops. As the Indians tried to abandon the fight and escape, government soldiers followed them and shot as many as they could. At least 146 (and maybe as many as 300) Indians died.

The massacre at Wounded Knee seemed to break the spirit of the Sioux. Scores of Ghost Dancers lay dead with bulletholes in their magic shirts. Even the few hundred warriors who remained in the South Dakota Badlands found themselves surrounded by immense numbers of U.S. soldiers. It took the government only a few more weeks to round up just about all the Sioux who were not yet on reservations. A formerly self-sufficient people were now virtual captives of the government, without either the rights of citizens or the independence of a sovereign nation.

The Southwest and California

In every region, Indians lost their freedom in much the same way. The Navajos, with their herds and orchards, were one of the most prosperous groups in the Southwest. But in the

Cochise

1860s, Americans began to insist that the Navajos move aside and surrender their land to whites. After resisting for several years, the Navajos finally gave in and were sent—under the guard of Christopher (Kit) Carson, a frontier fighter who had long harassed the Indians of the Southwest—to the Bosque Redondo reservation, a desolate tract in what is now New Mexico. Eventually, however, the federal government realized that Bosque Redondo could barely support human life, and the Navajos were allowed to return in 1868 to a reservation in traditional Navajo territory.

The Apaches were something else. They did not change their desert style of life and become herders or farmers. Instead, they hunted, mostly on foot, in the high, rugged mountains and arid deserts of their homeland. When the hunt yielded too little meat, they supplemented it by raiding the livestock herds owned by other Indians, Mexicans, and Americans. Tough and resourceful, the Apaches could survive under conditions that would kill most other people. They were not good candidates for reservation life.

During the 1860s, a Chiricahua Apache named Cochise showed U.S. troops how tough the Apaches could be. After he was falsely accused of various crimes, Cochise was driven to a life on the run. He and his followers lived by raiding farms and towns, and they held out firmly through a long hostage standoff and a subsequent war. Only in 1867 did he agree to give up fighting and move to a reservation.

By 1875, most of the Apaches had been placed on reservations, but keeping them there was another matter. Groups of dissatisfied Apaches slipped away from the reservations whenever they pleased and took refuge in the mountains, usually across the border in Mexico. The army spent a great deal of time and money trying to round them up. After enlisting Apache scouts to track holdouts in the forbidding mountains, the army had some success.

The last fugitive chief was Goyathlay ("One Who Yawns")—more commonly known by his Spanish name, Geronimo. At several times during the 1880s, Geronimo led groups of Apaches away from the reservations and into the mountains of Mexico or Arizona. They would live for a while by hunting and raiding, the army would capture them and send them back to a reservation, and then they would escape again. This cycle ended in 1886, when Geronimo finally surrendered for the last time and the Apaches were subdued. The survivors and their families were shipped to prisons in Florida, Alabama, and Virginia, where many died. Whites who saw that extinction was threatening the Apaches eventually arranged for them to return to their old reservation in Arizona. Geronimo's Chiricahua Apaches, however, were not welcome. The Chiricahuas were finally sent to the reservation of the Comanches and Kiowas in the Indian Territory. There Geronimo joined the Dutch Reformed Church (a group of Calvinist Christians) but was eventually expelled for gambling. As one of the territory's most highly publicized residents, Geronimo spent the last years of his life as something of a local curiosity, often visited by tourists or asked to appear at public gatherings. He died in 1909.

The Indians in California also had a history of displacement and mistreatment. In 1834, the Mexican government disbanded the California missions and turned mission lands over to the Indians who worked them. This transfer allowed the Mexican government and

Geronimo and several other Apaches waited at Fort Bowie, Arizona, after their surrender in 1886. Geronimo was later moved to the Indian Territory.

unscrupulous white settlers to grab a lot of formerly protected land, but some Indians managed to retain ownership of lands that their families had cultivated for generations. Then, in 1849, Americans rushed to California in search of gold. The adventurers who crowded into California helped themselves to Indian land with no pretense of legality. Whites simply murdered or chased away the Indian owners of any property they wanted. The Indians who managed to survive ran away to the hills or worked as itinerant farm laborers, living in a state of semi-slavery. The "wild" California Indians —especially the quiet, mostly vegetarian people known as "Diggers"— were shot down by any white settler who had the notion.

Before the great influx of whites, the Modoc tribe lived near the rivers and lakes of northern California and southern Oregon. During the 1860s,

the Modocs agreed to go to the reservation of the Klamath Indians in Oregon. When the Modocs got there, however, they found that they did not get along well with the Klamaths. Moreover, the supplies they had been promised never arrived. A young Modoc named Kintpuash—better known as Captain Jack, a name given to him by the white settlers—then led a group of his people out of the reservation and back to traditional Modoc territory.

The Modocs asked for a reservation in their old homeland, but their request was denied. When the army tried to force them back to the Klamath reservation, trouble broke out. Some Modocs were killed by the army, and more than a dozen white settlers were killed by a small party of Modocs. Captain Jack refused to surrender any of his people to the army for trial, and the Modocs hid in a rugged mountain stronghold known as the Lava Beds. Later, Captain Jack and some other Modocs killed some whites who had been sent to negotiate peace. Because of their impregnable position, Captain Jack's little band managed to fend off the forces sent against them. After a siege that lasted several months, however, the Modocs were captured, and Captain Jack and three of his followers were hanged. The remainder of his group was sent to the Indian Territory, where they remained until 1909. Then the 51 surviving Modocs were sent back west to Oregon.

The Nez Percés

In 1877, the Nez Percé Indians, who farmed and raised horses in the green valleys where the present-day states of Oregon, Washington, and Idaho meet, were forced to exchange their homeland for a reservation in Idaho. They were preparing to leave when violence broke out between harassing, marauding whites and some of the Nez Percé warriors. One of the tribe's leaders at that time was Hinmatun-Yahlatkit, usually known as Chief Joseph. Rather than abandon their people to army justice, Chief Joseph and the other leaders of the Nez Percés

decided to flee to Canada, where the American soldiers could not follow. The Nez Percés marched across some of the most rugged terrain in North America and evaded, outmaneuvered, and outfought the many army units sent to stop them. Their stamina and resolve have amazed military analysts ever since. But it was all for nothing. In northern Montana, a few miles short of their goal, Chief Joseph and his followers finally surrendered. Chief Joseph could no longer stand to see his people dying of fatigue and misery. Most of the warriors were dead; many women and children had perished or were dying from gunshot wounds, hunger, and cold. Those Nez Percés who were still alive were sent not to the Idaho reservation as they had been

promised but to the Indian Territory, where the hot, alien climate and disease continued the destructive work the army had begun.

About 700 Nez Percés had set out on the long march towards Canada in 1877. Seven years later, the 287 who still lived were allowed to return from the Indian Territory to the Northwest. Some of them went back to their relatives on the Idaho reservation, but Chief Joseph and a few others were not allowed to return. They were sent instead to the Colville Reservation in Washington. Chief Joseph ended his days in 1904 without ever seeing his homeland again.

Allotment

The penning up of the western tribes was scarcely complete before whites began to crowd onto the Indian reservations. Government representatives were sent west to induce the Indians to part with more of their "inalienable" lands. Then, in 1887, Congress passed the General Allotment Act (also called the Dawes Act), which provided that tribal lands be parceled out to individual Indians.

On the surface, this seemed to be a reasonable and compassionate approach. Sincere people who supported this bill felt that the Indians would adjust more rapidly to being farmers if they owned their own land, just as white farmers did. Unfortunately, this belief was based on white, not Indian, cultural values. Most Indian cultures did not value private ownership of land as highly as European cultures did. To many Indians, it was more natural for the whole tribe—not individuals—to own the land. Allotting small pieces of land to individuals threatened to fracture tribal societies.

Land-hungry whites, however, were enthusiastic supporters of the General Allotment Act. They realized that, after each adult Indian had received the allotted 160 acres (about 65 hectares) and each child had received half that, an immense amount of Indian land would be left over for sale to whites. In 1887, American Indian tribes held 138 million acres (about 56 million hectares) of land; by 1932, whites had acquired 90 million acres (about 36.5 million hectares) of it.

Mounted warriors of the Nez Percé tribe, photographed in Idaho in 1906

2
A CENTURY OF SHIFTING WINDS

A Ute woman and her child

An Uncertain Status

When the 20th century dawned, most American Indians were confined to reservations that were much like concentration camps. Ever since the passage of the Indian Removal Act in 1830, Indians had been uprooted from their ancestral homes in every part of the country. A great many had been shot or had died from starvation, exposure, exhaustion, or diseases—such as smallpox or tuberculosis—unknown to them before the whites came.

The reservations and the lives of the people living on them were managed and controlled by the Bureau of Indian Affairs (BIA). The responsibility of the BIA was to see that the best interests of the Indians were served; the agency was also responsible for deciding what those interests were.

The BIA, however, was managed and staffed almost entirely by whites. It was subject to the white government and was influenced by other white institutions, such as churches and businesses. Not surprisingly, the bureau held that the best interests of the Indians would be served only when they became a part of the dominant society.

The goal of the BIA was to be accomplished by a policy of "coercive assimilation"—Indian society was to disappear in the American melting pot. The funds used by the bureau to achieve this goal were deducted from the sums owed to the Indians by the government. Like the Cherokees, who had paid for their own removal, tribes were paying for the destruction of their own cultures.

Although this assimilation policy sounds cruel and insensitive, many white Americans felt they were doing the Indians a favor by following it. Their pride in American culture prevented them from seeing that Indians might be just as proud of their own cultures. Certain Christians felt that they were saving the Indians' souls by wiping out Indian religions and replacing them with one Christian denomination or another. Many Americans saw immigrants from other nations eager to blend in with mainstream American culture and assumed that the Indians would be just as eager to assimilate. They failed to recognize a crucial difference: most immigrants had voluntarily associated themselves with European-American culture, but American Indians were having that culture forced on them in a land that had once been theirs.

One of the most far-reaching efforts to "Americanize" the Indians was the BIA's education policy. Small children were taken from their homes and sent to BIA boarding schools. Isolated from their families, the youngsters were not allowed to speak their native languages, which were the only languages most of them knew when they first arrived at the schools. They were forced to practice the religion of whatever Christian denomination was in charge at the school. The teachers in these schools were usually whites who had no knowledge of or sympathy for Indian cultures. In BIA schools, the children found their Indian heritage treated with disapproval and contempt. The object of their education was to train them for life in the European culture that was considered the American mainstream.

Commissioners of Indian affairs—the top officials of the BIA—launched especially fierce attacks on Indian religions. In areas over which they had jurisdiction, primarily the reservations, these BIA commissioners routinely banned dancing and other acts of religious expression by the Indians. The BIA's usual justification for such bans was a weak claim that the dances were obscene or dangerous.

Indians who resisted assimilation paid a price. Those who continued to

33

Back (left to right): Humphrey Escharzay, Samson Noran, Hugh Chee, Basil Ekarden, Bishop Eatennah, Ernest Hogee. Front (left to right): Clement Seanilzay, Beatrice Kiahtel, Janette Pahgostatum, Margaret Y. Nadasthilah, Fred'k Eskelsejah.

Above: New students arrive at the Carlisle Indian School in Pennsylvania in 1886. Below: The same students, four months later.

Standing (left to right): Hugh Chee, Fred'k Eskelsejah, Margaret Y. Nadasthilah (with hand on other girl's shoulder), Clement Seanilzay, Samson Noran. Seated (left to right): Ernest Hogee, Humphrey Escharzay, Beatrice Kiahtel, Janette Pahgostatum, Bishop Eatennah, Basil Ekarden.

practice native religions or those who kept their children out of BIA schools found that their supplies and funds were withheld. They had to comply or starve. The BIA's excessive regulations and prohibitions made reservation life intolerable. Indians could not even leave the reservations without permission. The only way for a reservation Indian to avoid trouble was to remain passive and inconspicuous.

Silent passivity must have been very difficult for Indians who saw corrupt BIA officials getting rich. The BIA was so poorly supervised that corrupt officials could easily cheat the Indians and the American public. The system of political patronage—by which BIA jobs went to the friends of politicians—loaded the BIA with unqualified and dishonest officials.

In 1902, a reform law reduced this corruption by requiring that all BIA employees except the commissioner and the assistant commissioner be civil service appointees. This meant that BIA employees would have to pass a number of tests to demonstrate administrative abilities. No longer could politicians simply fill the bureau with their incompetent friends. Unfortunately, however, the aims and policies of the bureau did not change. BIA employees were more honest, but the Indians still suffered under a program of unwise policies.

At this point in history, many American Indians—especially those on reservations—held an unusual political status. These Indians were under the control of the U.S. government, but they were not U.S. citizens. When the United States government made treaties with the Indians in the 19th century, it acknowledged them as sovereign peoples. Sovereignty for the Indians in the United States, however, was always incomplete. It certainly did not mean that the Indians were free to build their own way of life and determine their own future. The U.S. Supreme Court usually referred to the Indian tribes with such phrases as "domestic dependent nations" and "wards of the government."

With the United States government's decision in 1871 to stop making treaties with the Indians and to stop considering them sovereign nations, an interesting question arose: if they were not separate nations, what were they? Some Indians had earlier become U.S. citizens by separating themselves from their tribes, by accepting land allotments under the Dawes Act, or through special agreements with the government. Many Indians, however, were not citizens of the United States. Since they were not citizens, they were largely unable to influence the decisions that the government made regarding Indian land and Indian lives. Between 1890 and 1920, Indians on the reservations were almost like prisoners of war, controlled by a government in which they had no voice.

But times changed. During World War I, thousands of Indians volunteered for the armed forces, even though, as noncitizens, they were not subject to the draft. The veterans of this war were rewarded later with a grant of U.S. citizenship. A few years after the war, power began to flow back into Indian hands. This was not the fully sovereign power Indians had enjoyed before contact with Europeans but, rather, political power that would begin to bring much-needed change and reform. A major step forward came in 1924, when the U.S. Congress passed the Indian Citizenship Act. This law granted U.S. citizenship to all Indians born in U.S. territory. (The right to vote, however, was withheld by some states until as late as 1948.)

The 1920s

Although prosperity came to much of America after World War I, Indians on the reservations did not share in the economic boom of the 1920s. Indian lands, however, drew the attention of land speculators and the developers of American industry. When oil and other important minerals were discovered on tribal lands that had once been judged worthless, whites once again pushed for the liquidation of tribal holdings.

In the 1920s, a major conflict arose over the land rights of the Pueblo Indians in New Mexico. After New Mexico became a state in 1912, the legal ownership of much of the Pueblo land became confused. To settle the matter, one of the new state's senators in Washington, D.C., proposed a law that would have forced Indians—not whites—to prove ownership of any disputed land. A white settler, even one who had simply occupied the land without permission, would be assumed to legally own the land unless an Indian could prove otherwise.

The Pueblos—and a number of whites who considered this proposal unjust—managed to stop it before it became law. The effort to stop this law brought the Pueblos together into an All-Pueblo Council in 1922. This council, the first joint Pueblo action since a revolt by the Pueblos against the Spanish in 1680, gave the Pueblos a taste of political power.

It also focused a lot of attention on the issue of Indian rights and how well the BIA was doing its job of protecting those rights. A non-Indian who was one of the nation's most vocal Indian-rights advocates, John Collier, said (loudly and often) that the BIA was not doing very well. Collier grew especially incensed when Charles H. Burke, the commissioner of Indian affairs, urged BIA officials to enforce the bureau's rules against religious expression by the Indians. Burke's reasons this time included a warning that Indians wasted a great deal of time and effort on these religious practices; their worship, Burke said, was keeping the Indians from getting their work done.

As criticism of the BIA grew more intense through the 1920s, Congress could no longer ignore the situation. The Senate ordered an investigation into the Bureau of Indian Affairs. The Meriam Report, which detailed the results of the investigation, was published in 1928. The report, in describing the conditions of Indian life on the reservations, was especially critical of two facts—that the Indians were allowed no voice in the management of their own affairs and that the services being supplied by government agencies, especially in health and education, were inadequate. Other investigations during the 1920s and 1930s—including one conducted by the BIA itself—reached similar conclusions.

The Indian Reorganization Act

After the publication of the Meriam Report, piecemeal reforms, mainly in education, were begun. Then, in 1933, President Franklin Delano Roosevelt appointed John Collier to head the BIA. Unlike his immediate predecessors, Collier was a hard-driving reformer bent on radically changing the federal government's policies towards Indians. In 1934, the Indian Reorganization Act (also known as the Wheeler-Howard Act) became law and required many of the changes Collier had sought.

Besides relatively mild provisions for the support of Indian culture, the new law contained some controversial proposals to promote Indian self-government. It also officially ended the allotment policy set up by the Dawes Act nearly 50 years earlier. Collier had especially wanted to stop allotment, a policy that he thought was eroding Indian societies. He even wanted to bring back under tribal control most of the land that had earlier been allotted to individual Indians. The Indian Reorganization Act gave him only some of what he wanted. No new allotments would be made, but (contrary to Collier's original plan) the law would still permit Indians to inherit land that had earlier been allotted to individual Indians. Tribes would regain control over allotted land only if the individuals holding that land wanted to return it to the tribe.

Tribes were given the right to decide whether they wanted the Indian Reorganization Act to apply to them. The law provided that they could not be forced, for example, to go through the elaborate process of setting up a tribal government if they did not want to. More than 180 tribes voted to accept the provisions of the law, but 77 tribes (including the Navajos, a very large group) voted against it. Most of those who rejected the law were concerned that it would give the Department of the Interior too much control over natural resources held by the Indians. Although the Indian Reorganization Act did not solve every problem faced by the Indians, it did have some positive long-term effects. For example, many of the smaller tribes accepting the act might never have set up tribal councils if the law had not encouraged them to do so.

Other reform laws also were passed during the 1930s. One of them, the Johnson-O'Malley Act, provided federal funds for local and private agencies that were serving Indian needs. For example, public schools where Indian students were enrolled got financial assistance. During the administration of Commissioner Collier, 16 federally operated boarding schools were closed, and 84 day schools for Indian children were opened. With fewer Indian children being removed from their homes and their cultures, it was hoped, Indian traditions might grow stronger among the young.

Also during Collier's administration (1933-1945), the BIA promoted programs to help the reservations work towards financial independence, especially through the management of their natural resources. In the Southwest, restoration and conservation of overgrazed lands, herd management, and irrigation projects brought increased prosperity. Tribes with forest lands improved their techniques of selective cutting, reforestation, and timber marketing. Also, Indians who produced authentic handmade crafts were encouraged to sell them directly, not through white merchants, so that more of the profit on a sale would go to the maker of the item. These programs brought a new feeling of self-sufficiency to many reservations. An amazing 96.6 percent of the federal loans the Indians received were repaid on time.

Relocation

World War II marked another turning point in Indian affairs. Many Indians were drafted, but an unusually high number—about 25,000 Indians—volunteered. The labor shortage that followed the mobilization of United States troops gave about 40,000 other Indians an

John Collier

38

opportunity to find jobs in cities. They were able to earn more at these jobs than they had ever earned before. In the process, Indians learned more about white society, and whites who had never before met an Indian heard about life on the reservations. After the war, some Indians stayed in the cities and blended into white communities, but many others returned to the reservations and were inspired to work for better living conditions there. Veterans of World War II led the campaign to remove the voting restrictions placed on Indian citizens in Arizona and New Mexico.

This new activism, however, was offset by another result of the war. The cost of the war had cut into government funds intended for non-military purposes, including Indian-assistance programs. Conservative congresspersons who were still eager to solve the "Indian problem" joined others who were eager to cut the national budget. Together they devised new federal policies to settle all Indian claims against the government, to remove tribal lands from trust status and place them on the tax rolls, and to put an end to federal responsibility for supplying services to Indians. The decisions that emerged during this period were short-sighted and, for the most part, disastrous.

To realize the first of these goals, Congress established the Indian Claims Commission (ICC) in 1946. The commission was to judge all Indian claims against the United States government and to settle them with cash payments. These payments would end the Indian claims forever and also end government responsibility to those whose claims were judged fair. Indians filed 852 claims in all. But judging the merits of each claim was complicated and time-consuming. It often involved reconstructing a situation that had existed at the time a treaty was made, sometimes more than 100 years earlier. Testimony from anthropologists and other experts had to be prepared and heard. By 1963, only 122 of the cases had been settled. The ICC was disbanded in 1978, and Indian claims were redirected to the United States Claims Court.

A relocation program to advance assimilation and to improve economic conditions was another new effort. Between 1957 and 1966, about 50,000 Indians left their reservations and were relocated in cities. The relocation program seemed to be successful at first, but it eventually created problems. The jobs obtained for Indians in the cities were often marginal, low-paying jobs from which Indians found it hard to get promoted. These jobs also failed to train Indians in any specialized work for which there would be a high demand among employers. When the national economy slumped, as it did in the late 1950s, jobs as unskilled laborers were the first to disappear. Once out of a job, Indians found it very difficult to find another. Those who had done only menial work had few skills that could lead to other jobs. Indians were also the victims of race discrimination in the labor market.

Most relocated Indians were not prepared for living in large cities. In the cities, poor Indians gravitated to the cheapest and most run-down housing. Indian ghettos then developed with the usual problems of city poverty—poor health, poor education, crime, and alcoholism. As the interrelated problems of gang warfare and illegal drug peddling became more prevalent in American cities, urban Indians were drawn into these dangerous pursuits as well.

Poor education was one of the most serious problems facing urban Indians. Besides the usual faults of poor inner-city schools, other factors made education especially grim for Indians. Very few schools had any teachers or administrators who were Indians. Indian students consequently lacked role models, examples of academically successful Indians to look up to. Many educators in public schools also expected Indian students to do poorly, so they lowered their standards of academic performance for Indians. Indian students, bored and unhappy, reacted by dropping out.

Relocated Indians, separated from family and friends, missed the security of their home communities. A great many Indians gave up and returned to their reservations. Others moved back and forth from city to reservation in a

Mohawk high-steel workers doing girder work in New York City.

constant quest for work or for new opportunities. Some made seasonal migrations to the reservations to fish, hunt, or harvest wild rice. Because they did not stay in one place long enough to establish resident status, many were not eligible for government services either in the city or on the reservation.

In some cities, community centers organized and operated by Indians helped to provide cultural centers and places where Indians could discuss their problems and find help. But not many Indians ever became truly satisfied with city life. Consider the case of the Mohawks. The high-steel workers of the Mohawk tribe are prosperous; because they are skilled in doing a dangerous type of work, their services are in demand. A large community of Mohawks has lived in Brooklyn for years. The Indians seem to be as comfortable in the city as their white neighbors, but the center of their life is still their reservation in Canada. Wives and children of men who are working on distant projects go home to the reservation to live. Vacations and retirement are spent on the reservation, and after an urban Mohawk dies, the body is taken home to the reservation for burial. The high-steel workers may have found a place in the city, but they have not really relocated.

Termination

In 1953, the widespread movement for ending federal aid to Indians led the United States House of Representatives to issue a statement called House Concurrent Resolution no. 108. This resolution expressed an intention to "terminate" the special status of Indians as soon as possible. Like many government policies towards Indians, termination seemed sensible at first, but was deeply flawed. Applying the same rules to Indians as to other citizens seemed not only fair but also respectful of the Indians as equals. Supporters of termination claimed that Indians cut loose from federal programs

would finally be proud and independent. It did not work out that way.

Although the legal aspects of termination are very complex, the basic principle was that the federal government would stop recognizing a given tribe as a special group. The individuals within this tribe would become ordinary citizens of the state in which they lived. The special services that used to be supplied to the tribe by the federal government would no longer be provided.

The federal government drew up a list of tribes that should be terminated first. The tribes first chosen for termination—notably the Menominees of Wisconsin and the Klamaths of Oregon —were those considered most ready to get along without federal help. In the early 1950s, Congress would simply pass laws that terminated the federal relationship with one tribe or another. Later, in 1958, the policy changed so that termination could only be applied to tribes that agreed to it. Some tribes saw potential gains and decided to try it.

The Menominees offer a good example of the effects of termination. They were doing well at managing their forest resources, they had plants to generate electrical power, and they were already paying for a large share of the federal services they received. Overall, they were organized, productive, and relatively prosperous. Congress passed a law in 1954 saying that the federal government's special relationship with the Menominees should be terminated as of the end of 1958. Approval by the Menominees was not required.

The schedule set by this law gave the Menominees only about three and a half years to make the transition to an entirely new way of life. They would have to become ordinary citizens of Wisconsin. The state of Wisconsin ruled that the Menominee reservation would become a new county, and an enormously complex transition got under way.

Every state has its own rules governing such details as the proper construction of roads, the inspection of electrical wiring in homes, and even the process of getting a license to do business in that state. Suddenly, the Menominees had to learn all of Wisconsin's rules and follow them. This meant that countless structures on the reservation—soon to be a county— would have to be modified. Many Indian professionals who had been doing business on the reservation would now have to meet new licensing requirements.

Another hard blow was that the Indians would now have to pay taxes on their land. They would also have to pay assessments for services, such as road maintenance and police protection, that they had once provided for themselves. The Menominees could not afford to meet Wisconsin's standards for their electricity-generating power plants and their tribal hospital,

so they had to sell the plants and close the hospital. Even when the Menominees were able to make the necessary changes to their established facilities, the complicated process took far longer than Congress had expected. The 1958 deadline was laughably unrealistic. Several times, the Menominees had to request that the deadline be pushed back, and termination did not actually occur until 1961.

The Menominees tried hard to adapt to their new status, but termination was a disaster for them. The newly formed Menominee County became a pocket of poverty in northeastern Wisconsin, with many of the characteristic symptoms of poverty, including a high infant death rate, tuberculosis, and poor housing. For a long time, the county had no resident doctor and no high school. The Menominees, a formerly prosperous people, saw their standard of living plummet.

Indian leaders in other parts of the nation saw a terrible chain of events in store for prosperous tribes: success led to termination and termination led to poverty. Working hard might bring short-term wealth, but it would eventually bring ruin. Various Indian organizations, especially the National Congress of American Indians, spoke out against the termination policy. In 1961, at a special conference convened by the University of Chicago, representatives of 90 tribes drafted a resolution that included a condemnation of the termination policy.

Fortunately, the terrible effects of the termination policy were noticed even by white politicians. Although Congress continued to pass acts of termination even as late as 1962—and members of Congress occasionally praised the policy even into the mid-1960s—termination was eventually allowed to die quietly. Various governmental agencies simply stopped enforcing the policy. One by one, tribes that had been terminated by law in the 1950s persuaded Congress to undo some of the damage. New laws officially redesignated the tribes as social units and reestablished federal responsibility for services to these tribes. The Menominees were among the tribes in line for a change. In 1975, more than 20 years after the U.S. Congress had voted to terminate the Menominees as a distinct people, the Menominee Reservation was reestablished.

During the administration of President Lyndon Johnson (1963-1968), the War on Poverty provided new opportunities for Indians. In order to get funds from the Office of Economic Opportunity (OEO), development programs had to employ local personnel and management, which meant that programs to help Indians would have to have Indian input. Indians who participated in OEO programs had the experience, often for the first time, of deciding which problems to attack, of planning solutions, and of then carrying out the plans. Young Indians who had left their home reservations for training in administration and management often returned to their home communities to help operate these programs.

As an example, the Navajo Rough Rock Demonstration School, a Community Action Project established in 1966 with OEO funding, gave the Navajos a chance to put their own ideas about education into practice. Other Indian-operated schools modeled on the Rough Rock approach, many of them privately funded, eventually were established.

Throughout the 1960s, American Indians also pushed for the establishment of a university that would be controlled by Indians and would reflect American Indian culture. These efforts resulted in the founding of Deganawidah-Quetzalcoatl University (usually called D-QU) at Davis, California. D-QU began operating in 1971 and has continued to offer two-year college programs in such fields as appropriate technology, Native American studies, and computer science. The university is open to students of all ethnic backgrounds, but it emphasizes an awareness of American Indian history and social values. Named after both an Iroquois prophet (Deganawidah) and an Aztec spiritual being (Quetzalcoatl), the university attempts to bring together the traditions of both North American and Middle American Indians.

3
CLAIMING A BETTER PLACE

A tiny, drafty house on the Cheyenne River Reservation in South Dakota, photographed in the 1960s

An Unpleasant Picture

During the last quarter of the 20th century, living conditions for American Indians have been generally grim. In most states, the health care and other services that American Indians have received (both within and outside of reservations) have been well below the national standard.

According to testimony given in 1989 before the U.S. Senate's Select Committee on Indian Affairs, American Indians living on reservations are three times more likely than other Americans to die before the age of 45. Many of those Indians dying so young are afflicted with illnesses of the liver—an indication that alcoholism might contribute to their ill health. For Indians who are ill, health care is not always easy to find. In most areas of the United States, one doctor is available for every 1000 persons. On American Indian reservations, the average number of doctors per 1000 residents is only 0.7. In the Aberdeen service area (North and South Dakota, parts of Montana, and parts of Nebraska) of the Bureau of Indian Affairs (BIA), the average number of doctors per 1000 residents is even lower—only about 0.4. Also, because the number of patients per doctor is so high and because living conditions are somewhat difficult, reservations often have trouble attracting the best and most experienced doctors.

American Indians living on or near reservations also have a serious unemployment problem. According to statistics published in 1989 by the BIA, 40 percent of the Indian labor force in regions served by the BIA is seeking work but is still unemployed. This compares with an overall U.S. unemployment rate of about 5.5 percent. The Indian statistics get even worse—up to 48 percent—if persons who could work but are no longer looking for work are included in the number of unemployed people. This means that nearly half of the employable American Indians who are served by the BIA either cannot find a job or have simply stopped looking.

In many other areas of life—such as income, housing, and education—American Indians are much worse off than is the average citizen of the United States. The relationship between American Indians and the rest of American society is still unsatisfactory—not only to Indians but to other Americans as well. American Indians, however, resent being portrayed as permanent victims. While acknowledging their problems, Indians have been working through several channels to improve their conditions.

Defining the Place of Government

Although Indians do not want to remain dependent on the federal government, the government's influence on their lives is still strong. During the latter part of the 20th century, the U.S. government continued to have little success in improving its relationship with American Indians. New federal initiatives have been tried, but most have simply added to the already large pile of failed policies.

Almost every year through the 1970s and 1980s, American Indian organizations and their leaders called for the reform—or even the dismantling—of the BIA. In 1977, President Jimmy Carter attempted to give more government attention to Indian matters by creating a new post at the Department of the Interior, assistant secretary for Indian affairs. Placing the BIA under a higher-ranking official, however, merely forced critics of the BIA to aim their complaints a little higher.

The assistant secretary for Indian affairs in 1982, Kenneth L. Smith (a Wasco from Oregon), was denounced after his boss, Interior Secretary James G. Watt, proposed a plan to save money by closing some local offices of the BIA. In 1988, major Indian organizations called for the removal of the assistant secretary at that time, Ross O. Swimmer (a Cherokee from Oklahoma), because they opposed his plan to reduce federal control of Indian schools.

It may seem strange that Indians would want to *keep* federal administration of Indian schools. Many of those who wanted to remove Swimmer for suggesting an end to federal control had earlier praised him for proposing greater Indian control over their own affairs. Overall, Indians have demonstrated mixed feelings about the federal role. While Indian leaders have pushed for greater sovereignty for their reservations, they have been reluctant to give up federal support. Perhaps remembering the disastrous termination policies of the 1950s, such groups as the National Congress of American Indians have argued that Indians are not yet ready to take over the management of schools and other institutions.

Tribal governments on the reservations have also come under fire. Reservation officials are elected by the voting members of the tribe (or tribes) who live on the reservation. These officials are responsible for managing the reservation's internal affairs. A tribal government on a reservation acts something like a county government. It governs such activities as the operation of school districts, the distribution of social services, and the zoning of land for industry, commerce, or housing.

Serious charges of corruption have been leveled against some of these tribal governments by the American Indians they represent. In 1979, the Ojibways of the Red Lake Reservation in Minnesota rioted in an attempt to remove the tribal chairman, Roger Jourdain, because they felt that he was misusing his position. Two persons were killed, three others were wounded, and several buildings on the reservation were burned during the protest. Many of the dissidents—including their leader, Harry Hanson—were arrested, tried in federal court, and sentenced to prison for their roles in the violent protest.

One of the most serious crises in tribal government, however, arose about a decade later on the huge Navajo Reservation that lies partly in four states—Arizona, New Mexico, Utah, and Colorado. Peter MacDonald, the head of the Navajo Tribal Council and one of the most prominent Indian leaders in the United States, was suspended in 1989 by the tribal council and accused of corruption. Among the charges against MacDonald were that he had accepted bribes from companies wanting to do business on the reservation and that he had deliberately arranged for the Navajos to pay too much for a ranch so that MacDonald could collect a commission on the extra amount. MacDonald was found guilty by both a Navajo tribal court and a federal grand jury and was sentenced in 1991 to a six-year prison term.

American Indians express widely varying opinions about how much political independence Indian reservations should have. Some Indians believe that reservations should actually secede from the United States to become separate countries. Others support a system in which reservations would function like local units within a state. Still others would modify such a system in various ways to give reservations more rights than local governments usually have. This last type of system is the current arrangement; reservations are like counties in some ways but more powerful than counties in other ways. Not all Indians who favor such a system, however, are satisfied with the powers that reservations have been given.

Although the tribal governments have some authority over the reservations and what happens on them, the extent of that authority is not really clear. The U.S. Supreme Court ruled in 1978 that Indian courts did not have the right to put non-Indians on trial for crimes committed on reservations. The Supreme Court, however, did rule in 1982 that Indian tribal governments can tax non-Indian companies that get oil or minerals from reservation land.

Peter MacDonald

In the summer of 1989, the hazy division of authority among various governmental units led to a standoff between state police officers and the Mohawk Indians of the St. Regis Reservation in upstate New York. The Mohawks were incensed after more than 200 agents of the Federal Bureau of Investigation (FBI) stormed the reservation and closed seven alleged gambling casinos. The situation was so volatile that, for 10 days, New York

47

Little Six Bingo, operated by Sioux Indians from Prior Lake, Minnesota, is one of many Indian-run bingo parlors in the United States. Federal courts have ruled that Indians may offer higher bingo prizes than other bingo operators because state restrictions do not apply to Indians.

state troopers blockaded all roads leading to the reservation. Inside the reservation, the Mohawks voted to continue casino gambling despite the FBI action.

Even though casino gambling is illegal according to the laws of New York State, the Mohawks contended that state gambling laws do not apply on the reservation. Numerous precedents seemed to support the Mohawk position. Throughout the 1980s, Indian

reservations in numerous states earned a lot of money by running high-payoff bingo games. Indian bingo parlors were able to offer huge prizes—as high as $50,000—because several court rulings have held that state limits on bingo prizes do not apply on reservations. While casino gambling became more common on reservations in the 1990s, the role that state and federal governments should play in regulating these casinos remains unclear.

This is only one of many areas in which the division of authority among governments remains unclear. Because the law does not fully describe the limits of tribal authority, further court cases will almost certainly be needed to define the role of governments—federal, state, and tribal—in Indian affairs.

Organizing for Change

Besides the formal governments under which they live, American Indians have also looked for leadership to voluntary, nongovernmental organizations. These organizations have had a great impact, and their influence has been increasing.

Many Indian leaders have believed that true strength can only be found in a coalition of tribes. The most prominent American Indian organizations are pan-Indian—that is, they cross tribal boundaries and emphasize the solution of problems shared by numerous tribes.

In 1944, the National Congress of American Indians (NCAI) was formed. Although there are individual members in the organization, many of its members represent larger groups of Indians. More than 120 tribes have representatives in the NCAI. As one of the most influential of the pan-Indian groups, it played a major role in bringing an end to the U.S. government's termination policies. The NCAI has continued to specialize in influencing legislation that affects Indians and their relations with the federal government. Some of the strongest criticisms of the BIA's policies, especially those for reducing the federal role in Indian education, have come from the NCAI.

Another influential pan-Indian group is the Council of Energy Resource Tribes (CERT), a group formed in 1975. The number of tribes represented in the CERT stood at 44 in 1990, but this number is likely to increase as the value of energy resources—especially coal, oil, natural gas, and uranium—on tribal lands continues to rise. Even though Indian reservations were often confined to land that white settlers did not want, Indian lands have since been found to be rich in energy resources. The tribes in the CERT work together to set energy-use policies that will guarantee Indians a fair share of profits from energy extraction.

In 1968, a number of Indians living in Minneapolis, a city with a large Indian population, felt that Indians were being harassed and discriminated against by the Minneapolis Police Department. In response, they founded the American Indian Movement (AIM) and set up street patrols of Indian civilians in order to monitor the actions of the police. This was the origin of one of the most highly publicized, and one of the most militant, Indian organizations of the 20th century.

Indian militance—a willingness to resort to force and even violence to achieve goals—grew steadily in the late 1960s and 1970s. In 1969, Indians occupied the island of Alcatraz in California's San Francisco Bay. Alcatraz had once held a federal prison, but the prison was closed in 1963. The Indians who occupied it claimed that, since the federal government had abandoned the island, ownership of it had legally reverted to the Indians. The occupation of the island gained a lot of attention from the news media and lasted a little bit more than a year, but federal marshals removed the Indians in the summer of 1971. The property became a national recreation area in 1972.

The Indian occupiers of Alcatraz had set an example, however, that AIM leaders were quick to follow. AIM became involved in many high-profile Indian protests. In 1971, they took over an almost-deserted military facility at the Minneapolis-St. Paul Airport and demanded permission to use the facility as a site for a school. The leaders were arrested and removed from the site. In 1972, AIM activists led several hundred protesters in a march on Washington, D.C. They then took over the headquarters of the BIA to protest the bureau's ineffectiveness in helping Indians. The protesters were eventually persuaded to leave, but they took many of the BIA's Indian artworks and several BIA documents with them on their way out.

American Indian activists occupied Alcatraz Island from late 1969 to the summer of 1971.

As dramatic as these events were, they were just a prelude to greater strife. AIM leaders became involved in a bloody uprising on the Pine Ridge Reservation in South Dakota in 1973. The original issue involved charges that Richard Wilson, the president of the Oglala Sioux, had mismanaged the tribe's affairs. Soon, however, the protest expanded far beyond demands for Wilson's removal. AIM activists and their followers at Pine Ridge occupied the village of Wounded Knee, a highly symbolic location near where at least 146 innocent Indians had been killed by U.S. troops in 1890. In addition to their claims against Wilson, the occupiers of Wounded Knee called for a broad reexamination of U.S. government policies towards Indians. Federal marshals surrounded Wounded Knee. Periodic gun battles then broke out, leading to two deaths and several injuries. The Indians holding Wounded Knee surrendered after 71 days, and two AIM leaders involved in the protest, Dennis Banks and Russell Means, were brought to trial in federal court in St. Paul, Minnesota. Charges against them were dismissed, but trouble, including several more shootings, continued at Wounded Knee until a 1976 tribal election eventually removed Wilson from his post.

Despite these and other militant acts, AIM has also worked in more peaceful ways to improve the lives of American Indians. AIM set up the Heart of the Earth Survival School in Minne-apolis, a school where Indian children can be educated in Indian traditions while studying the subjects usually taught in U.S. schools. AIM began a peaceful protest against the names and logos of the Atlanta Braves and the Washington Redskins, names and images that many Indians find offensive to their people and heritage.

Trying the Courts

Land

Indians seeking to restore tribal rights to land have had some success by pressing their claims in court. The U.S. government has long recognized the need to somehow compensate Indians for land that was taken from them through treaty violations or other illegal means. From 1946 to 1978, a special government panel, the Indian Claims Commission, heard the cases of the Indians and tried to work out final settlements of land claims. This, however, was not an ordinary court. Some of its settlements satisfied the Indians, but many decisions made by this commission awarded the Indians amounts of money and land that seemed far too small. Because of this, many Indians were unwilling to accept the commission's decisions as final settlements. This is one of the reasons the commission was disbanded in 1978.

A tipi–a traditional Indian dwelling–stands in the courtyard of the Heart of the Earth Survival School in Minneapolis. This tipi was set up for a special school festival.

Many Indian claims pursued through the ordinary courts of the United States have been resolved more satisfactorily. One landmark case, filed in 1972 by the Penobscot and Passamaquoddy Indians of Maine, involved claims by the Indians that most of Maine had been illegally taken from them in the late 18th and early 19th centuries. Lawyers for the Indians pointed out that, according to a U.S. law passed in 1790, the state of Maine and other parties were not legally allowed to make land treaties with the Indians. Since only the U.S. Congress had the right to make treaties, all those old agreements were invalid and the land still belonged to the Indians.

This had major implications for non-Indians who owned land in many parts of Maine–or who thought they owned it. With their ownership of the land in doubt, these people would not be able to sell the houses or businesses that stood on this land. Still, the federal courts considered the Indians' claim legitimate and agreed to hear the case. With the possibility of a very long court battle ahead, the U.S. government negotiated a settlement with the Indians. The Indians would gain income from the interest on a $27 million trust fund, and the government would spend an additional $54.5 million dollars to buy a 300,000-acre (121,500-hectare) parcel of land to be given to the Indians. In return, the Indians agreed to consider this a final settlement and to drop all claims to the land that had been in dispute.

This case is only one of several such land disputes settled in court or by binding out-of-court agreements. Such Indian tribes as the Seminoles of Florida, the Narragansetts of Rhode Island, and the Cayugas of New York have received payment in a mixture of cash and land to settle their claims.

Not all Indian land claims, however, have been settled by such a formula. One especially difficult case involves the Black Hills of South Dakota and the insistence of the Sioux tribes, especially the Oglala Sioux, that this territory is sacred to them and must be returned. The U.S. Supreme Court ruled in 1980 that the federal government should pay the Sioux $122.5 million for the land, but the Sioux rejected the award. They have stated that no amount of money can compensate them and that only the return of the land will be satisfactory.

Not all of the disputes over Indian land are conflicts between whites and Indians. The Navajos and the Hopi Indians have argued for about 100 years over which of the tribes really owns certain parcels of land in Arizona. The U.S. Congress tried to settle things in 1974 by passing a law to divide the land into a Navajo section and a Hopi section. Anyone who lived on the wrong side of the line would have to move. Most of the people who would have to be relocated were Navajos, and the Navajo Nation protested the law. A federal court in 1982 upheld the law, however, and penalized the Navajos for refusing to obey it. Unhappy as they were about the decision, the Navajos agreed to abide by the law if the federal government would help pay the moving costs of those families who had to be relocated.

Resources

Other very difficult issues before the courts include Indian claims on natural resources. Especially in the relatively dry western United States, control of water is extremely important. In 1908, a Supreme Court decision held that Indians deserve special rights to use water. The Indians have charged, however, that their rights have been ignored as states have installed irrigation, hydroelectric, and water-intensive coal-mining facilities.

Other problems involve the hunting and fishing rights granted to Indians. In many treaties with the Indians, the U.S. government agreed to let the Indians continue to hunt and fish as they pleased not only on reservations but also in the areas granted by the Indians to the federal government. Non-Indians, however, have argued that such hunting and fishing by Indians would result in lower catches for non-Indians and might even seriously deplete the populations of some species.

In the state of Washington, a federal court ruled in 1974 that Indians of that state not only enjoyed the right to fish outside their reservations but also were entitled to half of all the catchable fish in areas that the tribes had occupied before the whites arrived. Whites were incensed and challenged the ruling, but the U.S. Supreme Court upheld it in 1979.

Most states have rules outlawing certain fishing techniques—such as the use of gill nets or spears—in order to avoid depleting fish populations. Indians, however, often enjoy rights to use such methods because to do so is part of their traditional tribal cultures. In many cases where Indians are exempted from the normal state regulations, whites have lodged strong protests. Each year, for example, when the Ojibway Indians of northern Wisconsin start their spring season of spearfishing, they are challenged by white protesters. Indians are also permitted to use nets in fishing on Lake Michigan, a practice that angers whites—who may use only individual lines to fish the lake commercially. Federal courts, however, have denied the state of Michigan the right to regulate Indian fishing methods.

Religion

Court battles involving the religious practices of Indians have also been very controversial. Each of the many Indian cultures developed its own religious system; no single, undivided "Indian religion" exists. Nevertheless, certain features are common to many of the religions traditionally practiced by the American Indians. One of these is the belief in a supreme spiritual force, sometimes called the Great Spirit. Another common belief is in the need to seek out one's own guiding spirit, a spiritual being who will help lead each individual through life. Many Indian traditions encourage people to seek greater contact with the spirit world through fasting, meditating, dancing, or using certain natural drugs.

Indian religions, poorly understood by white Americans, have long faced opposition. The BIA and many private white organizations often considered it their job to extinguish Indian religions and convert the Indians to Christianity. Many Indians *were* converted to Christianity, and virtually every Christian denomination counts some Indians among its members. Elements of traditional Indian religions, however, still survive—both in the private observances of small groups of Indians and in the beliefs of larger organized groups such as the Native American Church. These Indians, however, still face opposition because their ways clash with the beliefs held by most Americans.

A highly controversial Supreme Court ruling in 1990 held that states could legally prevent American Indians from taking the drug peyote for religious purposes. Peyote, made from the mescal cactus, has been used for centuries by Indians of the American West in religious ceremonies. The federal government and 23 states have special rules allowing Indians to use peyote in religious ceremonies even though the drug is otherwise outlawed.

Oregon, however, is not one of those states. Two Oregon members of the Native American Church were denied unemployment compensation by the state because they had been fired for using an illegal drug. The two men sued, claiming that Oregon was violating their constitutional right to "free exercise" of religion.

The Supreme Court's 1990 decision held that Oregon had not violated the men's rights. Justice Antonin Scalia, who wrote the court's majority ruling, said that Oregon had no obligation to allow the use of peyote. Scalia wrote that only two kinds of law could violate the First Amendment right to "free exercise" of religion—laws that purposely (not just accidentally) restrict religious conduct and laws that limit speech or the press as well as conduct. Even though the Oregon law had the effect of limiting religious freedom, Scalia wrote, the law was constitutional because this effect was not the purpose of the law. Four other Supreme Court justices disagreed with Scalia's reasoning, seeing it as a threat to the right to free exercise of religion.

Many American Indians also believe that their religious beliefs about how

A prehistoric Pueblo Indian burial site at Glen Canyon, Utah

to treat the dead are violated when museums display skeletons and other items from Indian graves. Scholars from universities and museums say that valuable archaeological evidence is lost when Indian remains are reburied. Still, several major collections—such as those at Stanford University and the Smithsonian Institution—have returned the remains of Indians for reburial at the sites where they had been found.

4
CONTRIBUTIONS TO AMERICAN LIFE

Charles Curtis, who was part Kaw and part Osage, served as vice president of the United States under President Herbert Hoover.

America's Oldest Traditions

The names of countless North American rivers, lakes, mountains, and cities come from one American Indian language or another. The American Indians, however, did not simply name places and move on. They had worked the land of this continent for tens of thousands of years before the whites arrived. Being intimately familiar with the land, the waters, the weather, the plants, and the animals of North America, the American Indians had much to teach the European newcomers.

The climate of North America appeared harsh to many Europeans, especially to those from maritime zones (where warm seas moderate the weather). Many English, French, and Spanish newcomers had never experienced such hot summers, cold winters, deep snows, prolonged droughts, or short growing seasons as they found in various parts of North America. Each American Indian tribe, however, had long been culturally adapted to the climate of its homeland. To survive in America, Europeans had to learn from the Indians how to build appropriate shelters out of materials such as logs, mud, or sod.

Thousands of plant products are now so much a part of other cultures that it is easy to forget that the American Indians had them first.

The crop known sometimes as maize but usually as corn is now one of the world's most important grains. At the time of the first European expeditions to North America, however, only the American Indians knew of it. The Europeans learned from the Indians how to cultivate and cook with corn. The Indians of the Southwest also taught Europeans how to use another important plant, the potato.

A long list of other vegetables, fruits, and spices were introduced to the world by American Indians: tomatoes, zucchini, chili peppers, cranberries, maple syrup, and countless varieties of beans, squashes, and berries.

Government and Public Affairs

Long before any European ever set foot on North American soil, a democratic government was operating in the New World. This was the Iroquois League—a confederation of the Cayuga, Mohawk, Oneida, Onondaga, and Seneca peoples of what is now New York State (and, later, also the Tuscarora Indians who had fled North Carolina). The league offered an example of how tribes could rule their own affairs yet get together to take care of issues that concerned them all. The Iroquois League used a federal organization—a system in which a central government exercises some power but the state (or tribal) governments keep a great deal of authority over their own affairs. The league was, in many ways, an earlier version of the system eventually chosen for the United States government. Many of the founders of the United States had studied the Iroquois League's system of government, and they may have had the Iroquois model in mind as they constructed the U.S. federal system.

Other Indian tribes in North America also had advanced systems of government. Some degree of democracy was not at all unusual among American Indians. Many tribes were organized so that a primary leader had to answer to a council or an advisory board representing the members of the tribe.

Many Indians, after becoming citizens of the United States, were merely carrying on an Indian tradition by getting involved in politics.

Many of the American Indians most prominent in government have come from Oklahoma. One factor in this is the sheer size of the Indian population in that state. (Oklahoma has the largest number of residents reporting at least some American Indian ancestry.) Another factor is that many of the tribes forced to move to the Indian Territory, such as the Cherokees, had long experience with representative forms of government.

Robert Owen (1856–1947), a Cherokee, was one of the first two U.S. senators elected from Oklahoma after the state was established in 1907. He had practiced law in the Indian Territory before statehood, and he had organized the First National Bank of Muskogee in 1890.

William W. Hastings (1866–1938), also a Cherokee, was another early representative to Congress from Oklahoma. He received a degree in law from Vanderbilt University, and he was admitted to the bar in 1889. Hastings served as attorney general for the Cherokee Nation from 1891 to 1895 and as national attorney for the tribe from 1907 to 1914. In the latter capacity, he represented the Cherokees in Washington, D.C., in their dealings with the federal government. He served in the U.S. House of Representatives from 1915 to 1921 and again from 1923 to 1935.

Charles Carter (1858–1929), a Choctaw, represented Oklahoma in the United States House of Representatives from 1907 to 1927. William G. Stigler, also a Choctaw, was another U.S. congressperson born in the Indian Territory. After practicing law for a while in Oklahoma, he was elected to the House of Representatives in 1944. He served there until his death in 1952.

Oklahoma, of course, was not the only state to produce prominent American Indian politicians. The highest-ranking political officeholder to claim Indian blood was Charles Curtis (1860–1936) of Kansas. He was descended, through his grandmother, from Kaw and Osage chiefs. Curtis became a member of the U.S. House of Representatives from Kansas in 1892 and was elected to the U.S. Senate in 1907. After serving as senate majority leader, he became the Republican candidate for vice president on Herbert Hoover's presidential ticket in 1928. Curtis served as vice president of the United States under President Hoover from 1929 to 1932.

Benjamin Reifel, a Rosebud Sioux, was elected to the United States House of Representatives from South Dakota in 1960. During his term, he was the only Indian in Congress. Reifel became the ranking minority member of the House Appropriations Committee and served in the House until 1970. In 1976, he was appointed temporary acting commissioner of the Bureau of Indian Affairs (BIA).

Ely S. Parker

Ely S. Parker (1828–1895) was a versatile leader who broke much new ground for American Indians in government service. Parker, a Seneca from the Tonawanda Reservation in New York State, came from one of the Seneca tribe's most prominent families. He became a *sachem*–a member of the Seneca governing council–in 1852. Parker attended a missionary school and studied law, but he was not admitted to the New York bar because of his race.

When he realized that a career in law was closed to him, Parker turned to engineering. He studied at the Rensselaer Polytechnic Institute in Troy, New York, and, after receiving an engineering degree, worked on the Erie Canal for the United States government. He was promoted to the position of superintendent of construction at Galena, Illinois, in 1857.

While at Galena, Parker became acquainted with Ulysses S. Grant. When the Civil War began, Parker volunteered his services to the Union Army. Someone with Parker's education and experience would ordinarily have been commissioned as an officer, but Parker was denied an officer's rank because of his race. Only after General Grant had lobbied long and hard on his behalf did Parker finally receive a commission, as a captain of engineers, in 1863.

In 1864, Parker became Grant's military secretary and a lieutenant colonel. It was Parker who drafted the final terms of surrender signed by Confederate General Robert E. Lee at Appomattox Court House, Virginia, in 1865. Parker was promoted to brigadier general in 1867, but his career turned more to administration than to military duties. Parker served on several U.S. government commissions attempting to resolve problems with the Indians of the Great Plains. Then Ulysses S. Grant became president in 1869. Grant, who greatly respected Parker's judgment, picked Parker to head the BIA. For the first time since its establishment in 1824, the BIA had an American Indian as its commissioner.

Parker became commissioner of Indian affairs at a critical time in the relationship between the government and the Indians of the American West. According to a vaguely defined "peace policy," most of the U.S. officials involved with Indian affairs thought it would be best to put Indians on reservations and to send in teachers and other persons who would "civilize" and Christianize the Indians. Parker agreed with this policy. Parker also wanted the government to stop making treaties with the Indians as if they were sovereign peoples; he considered these treaties, which were often broken within months of their signing, cruel hoaxes. It was in 1871, during Parker's tenure as commissioner, that Congress passed a law doing just that—ending the policy of writing treaties with Indians.

Corruption was another major issue at the time of Parker's leadership of the BIA. *Indian rings*—conspiracies of BIA officials, providers of supplies, and unscrupulous characters in several other positions—were widely assumed to have banded together to systematically profit by cheating the Indians of promised supplies. Such rings of corrupt officials were probably less well organized than most people thought, but fraud was common enough that it was difficult for any BIA official to avoid being suspected of it.

Rumors that Parker was part of an Indian ring eventually spread. These rumors were his eventual undoing when, in order to offer quick relief to starving Indians on the Great Plains, he authorized the emergency shipment of supplies to these Indians—without taking the usual competitive bids from prospective suppliers of food. Parker's enemies accused him of improper purchases, and there was a congressional investigation of his administration. Although Parker was cleared of all charges, he had become so controversial that he felt he could no longer be of any use to either the Indians or the government. He resigned his position in 1871.

For nearly a century afterwards, all of the commissioners of Indian affairs were whites. Finally, in 1966, Robert L. Bennett, an Oneida from Wisconsin who had been a BIA official since 1933, was appointed to head the BIA. Since that time, all of the highest-ranking Indian-affairs officers in the federal government have been American Indians. Those after Bennett who served as commissioner of Indian affairs were Louis R. Bruce (an Onondaga) from 1969 to 1973, Morris Thompson (Athapascan) from 1973 to 1976, and Benjamin Reifel (Rosebud Sioux) as an interim acting commissioner in 1976 and early 1977. In 1977, President Jimmy Carter reorganized the Department of the Interior to create a new post, assistant secretary for Indian affairs, as the top federal Indian-affairs position. The American Indians who then served as assistant secretary for Indian affairs were Forrest J. Gerard

LaDonna Harris

Americans for Indian Opportunity. In 1951, Annie Wauneka became the first woman to be elected to the Navajo Tribal Council. As head of the council's health committee, she worked to reduce the high incidence of tuberculosis among the Navajos. In 1963, she was awarded the highest civilian honor in the United States, the Medal of Freedom.

Numerous major leadership positions in the late 1980s and 1990s were held by American Indian women. Wilma P. Mankiller became principal chief of the Cherokee Nation in 1985, the first woman to head such a large tribe. Susan Shown Harjo was executive director of the NCAI in the late 1980s and was succeeded in 1990 by another woman, A. Gay Kingman, a Cheyenne River Sioux.

(Blackfoot) from 1977 to 1980, Thomas Fredericks (Mandan and Hidatsa) from 1980 to 1982, Kenneth L. Smith (Wasco) from 1982 to 1985, Ross O. Swimmer (Cherokee) from 1985 to 1990, and Eddie F. Brown (Yaqui), who took office in 1990.

American Indian women have been among the foremost leaders in tribal government and in pan-Indian causes. LaDonna Harris, who grew up in the home of her Comanche grandparents, was the founder and first president of Oklahomans for Indian Opportunity and helped organize a group called

The Military

Some of America's most outstanding military leaders and heroes have been American Indians. During the Civil War, the Confederacy actively sought the support of the southeastern tribes—such as the Choctaws, Creeks, and Cherokees—transported west to the Indian Territory. Although some Indians felt that the wisest course was to stay out of the conflict altogether, eventually the Cherokees joined the Confederacy—even though the Indian Territory technically lay outside Confederate boundaries.

Stand Watie (1806-1871), a Cherokee, was given command of a regiment of volunteers known as the Cherokee Mounted Rifles. Clement Vann Rogers, the father of Will Rogers, was a member of this unit. Watie finally attained the highest rank held by any Indian in the Confederate Army—brigadier general —and was one of the last Confederate officers to surrender.

The highest-ranking American Indian in American military history was another Cherokee from Oklahoma, Admiral Joseph J. Clark (1893-1971). Clark was the first Indian ever admitted to the United States Naval Academy at Annapolis, Maryland. He served at sea during World War I, and, during the 1920s, went on to train as a naval aviator. Early in World War II, Clark served in the Mediterranean and the Pacific. He was captain of the aircraft carrier *Yorktown*, which was later sunk in the Battle of Midway in the Pacific. He was given command of its successor ship in 1943. Clark became a rear admiral in 1944.

Clarence Tinker (1887-1942), an Osage, also made a great contribution to the American effort in World War II. Tinker began his military career in the regular army, but he soon developed an interest in aircraft. In 1926, he became a member of the Army Air Force. In that same year, Tinker was awarded the Soldier's Medal for his efforts in saving a passenger from a burning plane. After the Japanese attack on Pearl Harbor in 1941, Tinker was given command of air force operations in Hawaii and the rank of major general. It was he who planned the use of American planes in the Pacific. He was a part of the American force that engaged the Japanese in the Battle of Midway, one of the great battles of history and a turning point in the war in the Pacific. During the battle, Tinker and his flight crew of eight were among the many Americans killed. Tinker Air Force Base in Oklahoma is named in his honor.

The United States Marine Corps during World War II recruited one of the most unusual communications units in U.S. history, a group of radio operators who were all Navajo Indians. This communications unit, often called the Code Talkers, would use their native Navajo language to communicate information vital to the Allied campaign in the South Pacific. The Japanese who intercepted these messages had no idea how to interpret the Navajo language—and probably never realized until after the war that what seemed to be an unbreakable artificial code was really a natural language. The Navajo Code Talkers were able to send messages that were as secure as any coded radio message but without the great expense of time normally required for encoding and decoding messages.

Ira B. Hayes, a Pima, was one of the U.S. Marines who took part in the Battle of Iwo Jima and who were photographed raising the American flag on Mount Suribachi. The photograph caught the imagination of the American people and was reproduced many times. It appeared on a postage stamp and finally served as the model for a bronze monument in Arlington (Virginia) National Cemetery to the Marine veterans of all American wars.

The soldiers in the photo who survived the battle were returned to the United States and entertained and honored as heroes from coast to coast. But when the spotlight faded, the public forgot Ira B. Hayes. In 1955, many Americans were shocked to learn that Hayes, at only 30 years of age, had

Ira B. Hayes, posing at right with para-chuting equipment, was one of the Marines raising the U.S. flag over Mount Suribachi (below) in World War II.

died of conditions that were probably brought on by alcohol abuse.

Arts and Crafts

In the early decades of the 20th century, the Southwest became the center of much pioneering work in American archaeology and anthropology. The discovery of prehistoric pottery, murals, and other artifacts drew many art afficionados to Santa Fe, New Mexico, and the surrounding area. Partially because of this widespread interest, New Mexico's Indians were encouraged to revive many traditional crafts. Indians soon found that outsiders were willing to pay for their creations, so they had an economic incentive to practice traditional arts and crafts.

Maria Martinez, a potter of the San Ildefonso Pueblo, was one of the best-known Indian artists of all. She had learned pottery-making from her aunt, who made and decorated pottery for use in her own household. When a museum began an archaeological dig at a site near San Ildefonso, Maria's husband Julian went to work there. Eventually the museum staff learned of Maria's skill and asked her to try to produce some pots like those that had been found at the dig. The only clues to construction and design were scattered shards that the archaeologists had found. Maria modeled the pots, and Julian painted them. Eventually, Maria and Julian developed a distinctive black-on-black pottery style.

Oscar Howe, a Yankton Sioux, is another well-known artist and illustrator. His murals decorate several public buildings in Illinois, Nebraska, and South Dakota. From 1948 to 1972, Howe was the designer of the giant murals decorating the exterior of the Corn Palace in Mitchell, South Dakota. These murals, which have to be replaced occasionally, are elaborate mosaics made entirely of multicolored corn kernels. Howe also illustrated a number of books about Indians.

Literature

American Indians also bring their talents to other art forms. N. Scott Momaday, part Kiowa and part Cherokee, won the Pulitzer Prize for fiction for his novel *House Made of Dawn* (published in 1968). In 1969 he also published *The Way to Rainy Mountain*, which is a retelling of Kiowa folktales accompanied by illustrations drawn by Momaday's father, Alfred Momaday. N. Scott Momaday is also a scholar of literature and has taught at such schools as Stanford University and the University of Arizona.

One of the most critically acclaimed American authors to emerge in the 1980s is Louise Erdrich, whose ancestry is half German and half Ojibway. Born in 1954, Erdrich grew up near the Turtle Lake Ojibway Reservation in

North Dakota. Even though she did not live on the reservation, her connections to it were strong. Both of her parents worked for the Bureau of Indian Affairs, and her maternal grandmother, whom she often visited, lived on the reservation. Erdrich drew on her experiences in and near the reservation in her later poems and novels. Her first major novel, *Love Medicine*, won a National Book Critics Circle Award in 1984. Later novels, *The Beet Queen* (1986) and *Tracks* (1988), continued to concentrate on the interactions between whites and Indians in North Dakota and Minnesota.

Erdrich's strong identification with American Indian concerns goes beyond her novels as well. Her husband, Michael A. Dorris, is one of the nation's most prominent American Indian scholars. Dorris, who is part Modoc, was born in 1945 in Dayton, Washington, and chairs the Native American Studies Department at Dartmouth College in New Hampshire. Besides his anthropological books and essays about American Indian issues, he has also published a novel, *A Yellow Raft in Blue Water* (1987).

Louise Erdrich

Music and Dance

Two members of the same Osage Indian family have become prominent in the world of the dance—Maria and Marjorie Tallchief. Maria Tallchief's career was shaped by her association with the famous choreographer George Balanchine, to whom she was married during part of her career with the New York City Ballet. Marjorie Tallchief was best known as a solo ballerina with the Paris Opera Ballet Company.

Among the ballets performed by Marjorie Tallchief was *Koshare*, one of three ballets written by the great composer Louis W. Ballard. Of Quapaw and Cherokee descent, Ballard has also composed numerous symphonic works and concertos with Indian themes.

Maria Tallchief

Buffy Sainte-Marie, a Cree folksinger and poet, enjoyed considerable popularity in the late 1960s and early 1970s. Many of her songs protest injustices suffered by Indians in America. She often performed on the award-winning *Sesame Street* television series, and she used her influence to promote the hiring of Indian performers on television.

Of the many American Indian rock musicians, the guitarist Link Wray has been one of the most influential. Wray, who is half Shawnee, recorded many electric-guitar instrumentals in the 1950s and 1960s, including the classic "Rawhide." The rhythms and textures in Wray's guitar work were unconventional, but they inspired later masters of the electric guitar such as Eric Clapton.

Sports

In the 1912 Olympic Games in Stockholm, Sweden, an American Indian was one of the brightest stars. Jim Thorpe—an Oklahoma Sauk and Fox and a football star at the Carlisle Indian School—became the first person in history to win both the decathlon and pentathlon events. King Gustav V of Sweden called him "the greatest athlete in the world." Unfortunately, Thorpe was not allowed to keep the Olympic gold medals he had won because he had been paid for playing baseball. His record, however, could not be taken away.

In 1920, Thorpe helped organize the Professional Football Association, which became the National Football League in 1922. He played for the Canton Bulldogs in Ohio and for the New York Giants. A 1950 poll of Associated Press sports writers named Thorpe the greatest male athlete of the first half of the 20th century.

At the 1964 Olympic Games in Tokyo, for the first time ever, an American runner won a gold medal in the 10,000-meter race. The athlete was Billy Mills, an Oglala Sioux who had been born in 1938 in South Dakota. Mills had run track and cross-country at the Haskell

Institute and the University of Kansas before joining the U.S. Marine Corps, in which he was serving at the time he won his Olympic gold. He was inducted into the National Track and Field Hall of Fame in 1976. Mills had also long shown an interest in public service, and he served as an assistant to the commissioner of Indian affairs from 1971 to 1974. After going into the insurance business in California, Mills became active in programs to help improve the social position of Indians. His accomplishments were portrayed in a 1983 film called *Running Brave*.

Entertainment

One of the most often-quoted American humorists, Will Rogers (1879-1935), was born in the Indian Territory to a prosperous and prominent Cherokee family. He resisted his family's attempts to make him a cattle baron and finally left school to work for several years as a cowboy. Rogers then left the United States and went to South Africa to herd cattle. When he found himself stranded there with very little cash, he joined Jack's Wild West Show to earn passage home. He was billed as "The Cherokee Kid—the Man Who Can Lasso the Tail of a Blowfly."

With this role, Rogers began an entertainment career that would be remembered many decades after his death. To spice up his performance in the show, he added humorous remarks

Jim Thorpe

to his rope tricks, and he then went on to become a success in vaudeville shows. He joined the Ziegfeld Follies in 1916.

Rogers then went to Hollywood. He enjoyed a modest success in silent pictures, but when sound films were introduced, his career took off. In such films as *David Harum* and *A Connecticut Yankee in King Arthur's Court,* he displayed the dry, folksy, low-key delivery that made his humor so popular. He amused his huge audiences by deflating the powerful and prestigious. In 1935, Rogers was killed in a plane crash near Point Barrow, Alaska.

Will Rogers

Another well-known American Indian entertainer was Jay Silverheels (1920-1980). A Mohawk whose family included many high-steel workers, Silverheels began his entertainment career in such movie westerns as *Broken Arrow* and *Brave Warrior*. In 1949, he began his best-known role—as Tonto in the *Lone Ranger* television series. During the 1960s, Silverheels founded the Indian Actors Workshop in Hollywood to help Indians get work in movies and television. In 1979, Silverheels was honored with a star in Hollywood's Walk of Fame, a section of sidewalk along Hollywood Boulevard in which the names of great entertainers are inscribed.

American Indians have contributed greatly to life in the United States, but Indians continue to seek a stronger, more equitable position in American society. If they attain it, other Americans can expect a way of life that is enriched even further by the classic traditions and modern achievements of the American Indians.

INDEX

ACKNOWLEDGMENTS The photographs in this book are reproduced through the courtesy of: p. 2, Utah State Historical Society; p. 6, Alaska Division of Tourism; p. 8, Montana Historical Society; pp. 11, 23, 24, 31, Smithsonian Institution National Anthropological Archives, Bureau of American Ethnology Collection; pp. 12, 67, 68, Independent Picture Service; p. 14, Library of Congress; p. 15, Woolaroc Museum, Bartlesville, Oklahoma; p. 18, Southern Pacific Transportation Company; p. 20, Glenbow Photograph, Calgary; p. 25, Western History Collections, University of Oklahoma Library; p. 26, Arizona Historical Society Library; pp. 28, 71 (left), U.S. Signal Corps, National Archives; pp. 29, 30, Smithsonian Institution; p. 32, "Ute Indian" by C. R. Savage, Church Historical Department, the Church of Jesus Christ of Latter-day Saints; p. 34 (top and bottom) Cumberland County Historical Society, Carlisle, Pennsylvania; pp. 38, 59, 63 (lower), National Archives; p. 40, Bethlehem Steel Corporation; p. 44, Bureau of Indian Affairs; p. 47, Peter MacDonald; p. 48, Little Six Bingo; p. 49, United Press International; p. 52, Heart of the Earth Survival School; p. 55, Department of Anthropology, University of Utah; p. 56, Kansas State Historical Society, Topeka; p. 61, Americans for Indian Opportunity; p. 63 (inset), Bureau of Indian Affairs; p. 65, Michael A. Dorris; p. 66, Library and Museum of the Performing Arts, Dance Collection; p. 71 (right), Vanguard Records; p. 72, Minnesota Office of Tourism Photo.

Front cover photograph by Susan Braine, Assiniboine Tribe. Back cover, top photograph: "Ute Indian" by C. R. Savage (top), courtesy of the Church Historical Department, the Church of Jesus Christ of Latter-day Saints. Used by permission. Back cover, bottom photograph: Bureau of Indian Affairs.

Stand Watie

Buffy Sainte-Marie

Don't miss the companion volume
AMERICAN INDIANS IN AMERICA, VOLUME 1
Prehistory to Late 18th Century

Groups featured in Lerner's In America series:

AMERICAN INDIANS   KOREANS
DANES   LEBANESE
FILIPINOS   MEXICANS
FRENCH   NORWEGIANS
GREEKS   PUERTO RICANS
ITALIANS   SCOTS &
JAPANESE   SCOTCH-IRISH
JEWS   VIETNAMESE

 Lerner Publications Company
241 First Avenue North • Minneapolis, Minnesota 55401